and Jimmy Durante and Helena Rubenstein for their help. Not to mention Mr. Tibor and LuLu and Alexander and my mother Sara and the mean lean Dean Lubensky machine. But finally and mostly, this book is dedicated to the delirious and hilarious Slutsky family, with loving memory of Yona.

and Igor Stravinsky Danny Kaye I want to thank for this book, up the name for thinking Schoenfeld K-k-kika my sister I want to thank laughs last. He who laughs last nuthin. nuthin equals Nuthin from

Published by the Penguin Group. Viking Penguin, a division of Penguin Books USA Inc., 375 Hudson Street, New York City, New York 10014, U.S.A. Penguin Books Ltd, 27 Wrights Lane, London W8 5TZ, England

Penguin Books Australia Ltd, Ringwood, Victoria, Australia Penguin Books Canada Ltd, 10 Alcorn Avenue, Toronto, Ontario, Canada M4V, 3B2. Penguin Books (N.Z.) Ltd, 182-190 Wairau Road, Auckland 10, New Zealand Printed in United States of A.

Designed by M&Co

10 9 8 7 6 5

First Published in 1990 by

Viking Penguin, a division of Penguin

Books USA Inc. ISBN 0-670-83545-5

Library of Congress Catalog

Card No.90-33044

MAX MAKES A MILLION

BY MAIRA KALMAN

viking

Call me Max.

Max the dreamer.

Max the poet.

Max the dog.

My dream is to live in Paris.

To live in Paris and be a p o e t.

Paris.
The city of dreams.
The city of lights.
The city of love.

But
do
you
think it
is easy
for a dog
to pack a
small brown
suitcase, put
on a beret,
and hop on a
plane? Ha! Plane
tickets cost
money. Mazuma, shekels,
semolians. I have none.
Because no one
wants to buy my
book. I'm flat broke.

Bone dry.

But someday,
fat families and
skinny families
around the world
will be reading my poems.
And laughing, and crying.
I feel it in my bones.

I want to say, before anything,
that dreams
are very important.

I

live

in New

York City.

That crazy

quivering wondering

wild city. A city like

an enormous orchestra.

A bebop city. Every-

one playing music that

screeches and slides

into my ears. Everyone

singing a different

song. Everyone

running a different

way. All day.

All night.

A jumping jazzy city.
Tall people.
Short people.

Plaid people.
Carrying boxes.
Carrying chairs.

Traffic. Towers.
A shimmering
stimmering

triple-decker sandwich
kind of city.
Wow. New York. Bow Wow Wow.

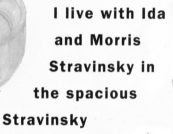

I live with Ida and Morris Stravinsky in the spacious Stravinsky apartment. Morris has a ladies' shoe store. Stravinsky Shoes. Every day he goes down to his store and shows women different shoes. Pumps. Sandals. Slippers. Mules. Morris and his assistant Laura are designing shoes for the Queen of Sheba, who must be a very fussy woman, because every time a customer makes Morris crazy he says, "Who do you think you are, the Queen of Sheba?"

ompadour   nuthin   schnozzola   luna   luckylemon

Meanwhile, across town,
Ida is taking tango lessons
with Maurice Chagall.

He has a big black shiny
pompadour on his head
and tiny
shiny
pointy shoes
on his feet.

Morris and Ida don't have any children.
But they have me, Max.
And they start to cry every time
I bring up the subject of
moving to Paris.
They will have to face the facts.
There is an old Chinese proverb that says
parents must give their children two things,
roots and wings.   I have the roots.

Now I want the wings.

Every morning I walk
downtown to my studio.
I pass the Gizmo Gallery.
I pass the Venus Beauty Salon
and Dance School. I daydream
and stroll and scribble
in my notebook. And every day
I pause on the corner of
Salami and Pastrami Street
and tape a poem on the wall.

People can stop
and read my poems
and then go on
their merry way.

I reach my studio,
the place I write.
I share my studio
with Bruno, my best friend.
Bruno is an artist.
He paints invisible paintings.

I met Bruno in the garden of the
Museum of Incredibly Modern Art.
He was holding a very
strange umbrella.
Maybe he thinks
the rain is invisible.

Ha!

Some people say,
"That Bruno is crazy."
But Bruno is
no crybaby.
He just keeps
working on   the ideas in his head.

If I didn't mention before,
I should mention now.
This book is about dreamers.
Wishful thinkers.
Dreamy blinkers.
Crazy nuts.

I go to my desk. A writer must write.
I close my eyes, say the first three
things I see, and write a poem.

Mrs.Hoogenschmidt

Fish

Mr.Hoogenschmidt

Saxophone

Nose

Glasses

It was on a sunny summer day that I met

Mrs. Hoo gen schmidt wearing a fish on her head.

dizzy fella

on his hands carrying an umbrella

Mr. Hoogenschmidt was walking

He meant to B**LOW**

the S**AX**O**PHONE**

the

but man,

he blew his

n
o
s
e

instead

and his glasses

flew off his head

onto the bed

Baby Henry's

The doorbell rang.
It was Baby Henry who owns
Baby Henry's Candy Shop.
Baby Henry travels to Turkey for
Turkish Taffy and to Cairo
for Caramel Camels.
Now he was having a candy dilemma.
"I need your advice," he said.
"Try these lemon drops from Nice.
Are they nice?" "Nice," I said.
"Twice nice," said Bruno.
"Good that it's nice," said Baby Henry.

I closed my eyes
while the candy lay
on my tongue.

Lemon groves. Full moon.
Sylvia's yellow dress.

I want to say
that wonderful ideas
can come from anywhere.
Sometimes you make a mistake,
or break something, or lose a hat, and the next
thing you know, you get a great idea. My idea was to eat.

Bruno and I left the studio. Walking to lunch
we passed the door of the mysterious twins
Otto and Otto
and their two dogs
Otto and Otto.

Tacked onto the quatro Otto door is
a note that toots in total rudeness and
which I reproduce in toto:

Pardon me means
excuse me.
Excuse me
means move.
Move means
GO AWAY.
GO AWAY MEANS
SCRAM AND
SCRAM MEANS
BEAT IT!

Bruno and Marlene are in love.
Did I mention that when
Bruno met Marlene he stopped
painting invisible paintings for
one week and painted only Marlene.

We reach the
Domino Luncheonette.
Marlene is waiting.
Marlene is a scientist.

She is studying gravity, which is why we
are stuck to the ground and not flying
off in all directions. Our waiter's
name is Marcello. He is an
architect. But no one will
live in his houses. He
only wants to build
houses that
are upside
down.

Marlene is worried that in a
house like that her skirt would
fall over her face and
she would be embarrassed.
"Wear pants, Marlene," says Bruno.

Walking back to the studio

we pass Princess Lenina

and her faithful horse Rex.

We pass Mr. Van Tiegham.

He is a musician.

He plays his drumsticks

on the garbage cans,

lampposts,

metal doors,

and building walls.

We watch as he disappears

down the street

hammering

and bangering

his zigzag

city song.

Ha!

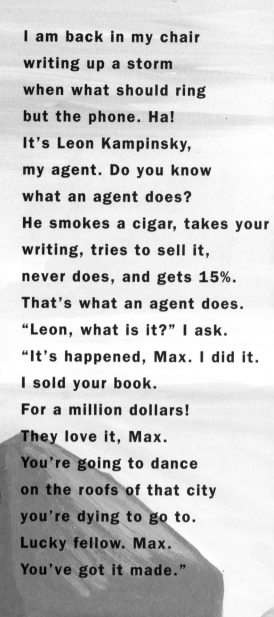

I am back in my chair
writing up a storm
when what should ring
but the phone. Ha!
It's Leon Kampinsky,
my agent. Do you know
what an agent does?
He smokes a cigar, takes your
writing, tries to sell it,
never does, and gets 15%.
That's what an agent does.
"Leon, what is it?" I ask.
"It's happened, Max. I did it.
I sold your book.
For a million dollars!
They love it, Max.
You're going to dance
on the roofs of that city
you're dying to go to.
Lucky fellow. Max.
You've got it made."

I got off the phone.
The black old phone.

Someone was going to print my book.
Someone was going to sell my book.
Someone was going to buy my book.

I couldn't talk.
I couldn't think.
I couldn't breathe.

The world was a fuzzy kind place.
The world was O.K.
Not just O.K. but A.O.K.
Bruno and I danced around.
Then I rushed uptown
to tell Morris and Ida.

They were
having a
party that night.
A musicale. A soirée.
I was going to recite my
poems. When I came home Ida
was frantic. "Quick, Max, start
making trays of canapés. Start
mixing martinis." "There's
something I have to tell you,
Ida." "Later, Max. Later. We
have guests coming. I have
to get dressed." I filled
platters with pomegranates
and figs. Bowls of olives
and baskets of tangerines.
My feet were rubbery.
My head was hot.
This was too much.
Too much for a
dog to bear.

The guests started arriving.

In walked Ivan Kazlinsky,
the arch rival of Leon Kampinsky.

"Ah, Max,"
sneered Ivan,
"still writing those
stupid little poems
that nobody likes?
Bring me a drink,
why don't you."
I was ready to rip the
pointy beard right off
his face. I was ready
to give his ugly pants
a bite so big, he would
be wearing shorts.
But instead I looked him
in the eye and said "Ha!"

And I secretly vowed
that Ivan Kazlinsky
would get his
terrible just desserts.

The party was a blur of perfume,
silk dresses, and laughing voices.
Ida said, "My dear friends.
Would you kindly take your seats.
We are ready."

It was mad.
First cousin Etta
swung on a trapeze
with her husband Little Socco.

Then
Rupert Mondasco
played the bagpipes
so hard
they exploded,
sending Helena Rubenstein's false
eyelashes flying off her face.
Bruno showed his paintings and
Princess Lenina bought them all.
"I love to see all this invisible stuff," the Princess explained.

Finally Marlene got up to explain gravity. "You see" she said, tossing three lemon pies into the air. "What goes up, m u s t come down."

And we all watched as
the three lemon pies
plopped, flopped, and dropped
onto Ivan Kazlinsky's

hairy
horrified
head.

Ha!
Ha!
Ha Ha!

It was my turn.
I shivered with fear
and excitement
and began to read:

I'm **gaga**
for a **saga**
of Ali **Baba**
and his forty **robbas.**

I'm **crazy**
to be **lazy**
with Sinbad
on his seven seas.

I want to dance
the **kazatski**
until I **plotski,**
and sing like a **boid**
on toity-toid and **toid**

Call me Max.
That lucky dog
with my dream shoes on

My life began
when I was **born.**
Hold the phone
I'll eat some **corn.**

Call me Max
that lucky dog.
With dream shoes
on my **feet.**
The world keeps
turning.
My shoes are **yearning**
to tapdance down
a lucky **street.**

The room was silent.
Then they all started to applaud.
"Max," they cried, "you are a
wunderdog, you are the funniest.
You are the greatest."

Dearest people,
How can I thank you.

This is the day
I have been waiting for
all my life. I am off.

Off to Paris to follow my dreams.
Be brave, Ida and Morris.
We will meet again
in that starry-eyed city.
You know I have always
lived by my dreams.
And now they have come true.
Roots and wings.
Roots and wings.
I've got to go,
Daddy-o.

So long.
Farewell.
Good-bye.

Ha!

'Allo? Allo Jacques?
Jacques, it is me, Mimi.
Oui. Oui. Mimi. I just got off
the phone with Kiki.
Oh Jacques, not Fifi, Kiki.
Listen. Zouzou called Loulou,
Loulou called Coco,
Coco called Kiki,
and Kiki called me me.
Have you heard the latest?
Tout Paris is abuzz. Max is here!
Who is Max??? Mon dieu!
Sacre bleu! He is the coolest cat,
I mean the hottest dog.
He is Max Stravinsky.
The dog poet from New York.
That bohemian beagle. He's
staying at Madame Camembert's.
I don't know what he's going
to do, but I will call Tarte.
Tarte Tatin. She finds out
everything from that bogus
Barcelonian baron,
Federico de Potatoes,
who is a fortune hunter or
a fortune teller or something,
but he is très intelligent and
he always gives her the scoop.
Alors, I must run.
My soufflé is sinking.
Jacques, there is something
in the air. Don't you think?
I feel it is very, oh so very . . .

Ooh-

First published in 1991 by Viking Penguin a division of Penguin Books U.S.A., Inc. Copyright © Maira Kalman 1991. All rights reserved cheri.

8 10
5 9 7
6 4
3

VIKING
Mon amour zis book eez published by that adorable Penguin Group Viking Penguin, a division of Penguin Books USA Inc., 375 Hudson Street, New York, New York (zat feelthy town) 10014, U.S.A. Penguin Books Ltd, 27 Lane, London-England Books Ringwood, Australia Books 2801 John Markham, Canada Penguin Books Wrights don W8 5TZ, Penguin Australia Ltd, Victoria Penguin Canada Ltd, Street Ontario L3 R1 B 4

Penguin Books (N.Z.) Ltd.

180-190 Wairau Road

Auckland 10

New Zealand

Penguin

Books Ltd.

Registered

Offices:

Harmondsworth,

Middlesex (ooh-la-lai),

England

The Library of Congress Catalog Card Number for this allergic book is 91-50209. ISBN 0-670-84163-3

Designed by M&Co. New York

Printed in U.S.A.

la-la

(MAX IN LOVE)

MAIRA KALMAN

For Venus,
Pluto,
and
T
i
b
o
r

Kalman

Mer
c i
beau
coup
to M.
Jacques
Tati and
mille fleurs
to Scott
Marquis de
Stowell

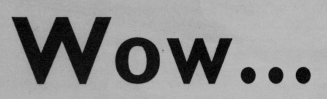

Wow...

Wow! **Wow!**

I can't believe it. Me. Max Stravinsky in Paris. Picasso. Pâté. The opera. Ballet. The crème de la crème. The city that gleams. That romantic, extravagantic city of dreams. Oh pluperfect Paris, just give me a chance and I'll toast your beauty, oh Paris of France.

Airport scene. Mad crush. Wild rush. Too much fame for this dog. I wanted to be alone.

My room was the Blue Suite
or as the French say,
"Bleu."

Bleu walls.

Bleu bed.

Bleu chair.

I was beat. I was bushed.
I lay down for a nap.
I dreamt that a bleu horse
was playing checkers
with a bleu woman
in a garden of bleu trees.

The sky was pink.

Go figure.

I was awakened by a k-k-**k**-**k**-knocking at the door.
In entered a

long mustache

followed by a man.

"Bonjour, Monsieur Max,
allow me to introduce myself.
I am Fritz from the Ritz
which I quit in a snit
when the chef in a fit
threw escargot on my chapeau
and hit my head
with a stale French bread.
Now I am here
in this little hôtel
run by the aromatic
Madame Camembert.
I adore her and
she adores me.
It's not always
that simple
in this town
of Paree."

With that, he placed
a tray on my bed.
"I thought you might
need this." He was right.
I was so hungry
I could have
eaten my beret.

As I was eating, my eyes fell on an amazing building outside my window.

"Fritz," I asked, "what's that scary looking shack with those creepy monsters sticking out?"

That *shack* monsieur, is the great Notre-Dame Cathedral and those 'monsters' are gargoyles. A hunchback used to live in that tower. And he died of a broken heart. And now I will leave you to your ruminations. Au revoir."

I gazed out the window and wondered.
About love.

The door, she knocked.
Entered a woman, walking a leopard.

"non"

"My name is
Charlotte Russe.
I came by autobus.
I am your French tutor.
But you are a chien! A dog!
Well never mind.
I have taught plenty of rats
in my time so I can
certainly teach a dog.
    Now. Put this clothes pin
on your nose,
make your mouth, ze bouche,
into a little bonbon shape.
    Put your hands on your hips,
stamp your foot and say, 'Non.
Non.Non.Non.Non.Non.'
Now say 'ooh la la.' That's it.
'Ooh la la and non.'"
Suddenly she flung
herself on the bed
crying, "Monsieur Max,
I cannot teach today.
I just fell in love and
I cannot concentrate."

With that she left.
What a lovesick town.

I was
itchy
to walk

through
the boulevards,
the parks, and
the little streets
on that
sunlit day.

To inhale leafy lilacy Paris.

It was April after all.

A baguette here,

a Napoleon there,

and I continued my ambling

around my

dove gray

debonnaire

town.

I decided I must see Mona Lisa, who is not a friend,
but a painting by Leonardo da Vinci.
Everyone in the world comes to Paris, runs to the museum,
stands on line for five or six hundred hours and then they all go
ooooh ooooh ooooh and ahhhhhh.

The funny thing is that some joker named Marcel Duchamp
decided that he would take the Mona Lisa and doll her up.
Which he did.
And people went ooh-la-la and ha ha ha.

As I left the museum,
I saw a scene that made my heart stand still.
A man had written poems all over
the sidewalk and the buildings and the cars
and the trees. As the cars left, parts of
his poems went whizzing around Paris,

and as the leaves fell from the trees, words fluttered down to the ground.

I kept walking.

I was in a funny mood.

Expecting something I couldn't name.

"Allo Jacques. It's moi, Mimi.
What a horrible day.
The butcher delivered
the wrong order.
Instead of sixty spicy saucissons
and a small steak
for my dog Sutzi
they delivered sixty steaks
and one sweet saucisson.
Then Louis L'Amour came over
and cried for three hours
about his beloved Lula Fabula
who ran away with the circus
to become a snake charmer.
Quelle kook.
But the latest on Max. He has
been seen everywhere with a
hangdog expression on his face
and if I know anything,
which I do,
this moody meandering means
one thing.
Love, Jacques. L'amour.
He is looking for,
needy of, and pining for love.
Lovelovelovelove is in the air.
Isn't it glorious, Jacques?
But I must dash.
My mousse is melting.
Byebye."

I had walked like crazy
when I suddenly came upon it.
It. The tinker toy tower.
The Eiffel Tower.

As I took the elevator up

up,

up

I looked

down

down

down

down
at the vista below, thinking of
the kings and queens, poets and
artists who had lived and loved
in this city. And I wondered
who invented the soufflé
anyway? And what
was he thinking?

A t-t-tap on my shoulder broke my reverie.
"Excusez-moi, but aren't you Max Stravinsky?"
"Yes," I answered brilliantly.
"I am Pierre Potpourri, the owner of the
Crazy Wolf Nightclub.
Monsieur Max, would you grace us
with your presence tonight
at the Crazy?"
"Yes," I answered dramatically.
"Capital. Now you must
join me for lunch.
I am meeting a
dear friend,
Madame
Melba."

The Peach. La Pêche. Everyone knew Peach Melba.
She owned the world famous
Glamour Puss Charm School.
She had two French bulldogs
on her lap who were having
a terrible argument
about philosophy.

"Idiote, imbécile, stupide!!"
they barked at each other.
Next to Melba was her
constant companion,
a monkey named Sammy
who was wearing
an enormous feather
in his hat which he used
to tickle people's ears.

"**Charrrrrmed** to meet you,
Mr. Shostakovitch," trilled
Melba as I bowed hello.
"Stravinsky," I said.
"The name is Stravinsky."
"Oh of course,
Mr. Stradivarius,
of course. Absurd mistake."

We all ordered soup du jour
and ate in peace until one
of the dogs dumped his soup
on the other one's head.
Lunch lunched, Melba toasted
we decided to go to the . . .

They had the most amazing hairdos from all these guys who flipped their wigs.

Pompadour Museum.

I headed back to the hotel.
On my way I saw
a pair of black shoes
sitting on the sidewalk.
Next to them stood
a fish-eyed man in his socks
looking up at the sky.

Back in my room,
the phone, he rang.
"Allo, zis eez
Monsieur Max,"
I said Frenchily.

"Hey, Max, what's with the phoney baloney French accent? It's me, Leon. Your devoted agent. While you stuff your face with french fries, I'm working like a dog making deals for you. And baby, this is it. The sweetest deal of all. I'm in Hollywood and they want you to write a script. Some cockamamie love story. They want you here pronto to start writing. You'll love it here. Everyone is beautiful. Love ya, Maxie. Ciao."

I hung up.
Leon sounded so
strange. The Cinema had
appeal. But something
was missing. How could
I write a love story if
I didn't have . . . love?

"Allo, alloooooo Jacques,
can you hear me? What is all
that wailing in the background?
Did you hear the latest? Max
had lunch with Peach Melba.
She runs that glamour school.
You must have seen her ads:
'Do Not Be a Sour Puss
Do Not Suck on Lemons
You Can Be a Glamour Puss
In a Makeover Made in Heaven.'
She charges an arm and a leg
and teaches people how to
dress walk talk eat breathe
and in the end, VOILÀ!
From a pig to a princess!!
Tonight?
I am going to the Crazy Wolf,
of course. Tout Paris
will be there. Max is coming.
Crêpes Suzette is performing.
Yes. That divine dalmation.
What will I wear?
You know that monkey, Sammy?
Yes, Sammy Lacroix. He is the
most brilliant fashion designer
and he has created this
fabulous frock made out of
bananas. Yes, only bananas.
But Jacques, I must run.
My bunches are beginning
to droop."

The night came.
Down and a flight of stairs
With stars.
a crooked
a crooked alley
I knocked three times
on a small green door
and I was in the Crazy
Wolf. That noise-soaked,
blue-smoked
spot.

Hey,
fermez la porte,
someone shouted.
Hey, fermez la
bouche, someone
else shouted.

Quelle
scene.

Suddenly a large wolf wearing a suit
came running toward me.
I nearly jumped to the chandelier.
"Max, it's me, Pierre,"
said the wolf, taking off his headdress.
"Welcome Max. We are about to begin the show.
Ladies and gentlemen, the
incomparable Crêpes Suzette."

All eyes turned
toward the stage.
The star-splattered,
peacock blue curtains
parted slowly.
A blue spotlight
curled down to
a black piano,
and there,
bathed in
that light,
was the dog
I had been
looking for
my whole life.

My insides were on fire.
I was smitten.
I was bitten.
I was in love.
She closed her eyes.
Her elegant paws with
her neatly manicured claws
began to play.
A Chopin ballade,
a smattering
of Smetana,
a medley
of Mozart.

As she finished,
the transported audience
burst into a frenzy of applause.
"Merci beaucoup,"
she murmured demurely.

I was clickering.
I wanted to run and hide.
The poem I had prepared
seemed meaningless.
CHAIRS? Who cared
about chairs? I tore up
the old poem and
jumped onto the stage.

Oh
my hootchie
kootchie
poochie
your hotty
spotty
body
makes me tingle with joy.
You played the legato,
my heart went staccato.
My musical muse
no longer confused,
I have found
my raison d'être.
It is you,
my Crêpes Suzette.

The rest, as they say,
is history. Crêpes is
coming with me to Hollywood.
She will compose
the music for my movie.
Our last day in Paris
we led the Dog Day Parade.
I read the poem I had
written for this occasion:
In chic Paree
the chicest day
is when the dogs stroll down
the Champs Elysées.
Great danes romancing,
pink poodles prancing.
It's swank
it's grand
it's pooch couture.
They saunter with style
about half a mile
and end up at Maxims,
that most marvelous spot
for champagne and caviar
and a little whatnot.
A toast to life
A toast to love
Salut! Olé!
We're off to L.A.!

"Allo.
Oh JacquesJacquesJacquesJacques
What a night it was.
Quelle nuit.
It was the night of love.
Before our eyes Max and
Crêpes became a dog duet.
Paw in paw they strolled
through Paris. But now,
they are sailing for Hollywood
on the Toujours L'Amour.
Oh Jacques, I feel so sad.
So empty. So triste.
Jacques, why do you never
say anything?
All I do is talktalktalktalktalk
to you and you hardly ever
utter a word and I . . .
What? WHAT??
Oh Jacques, I am stunned.
I am completely speechless
and I am trying to
think of something to say
but I cannot because
my mind is swirling and twirling
and . . .
What?
Yes Jacques. Yes. So simple.
Yes, of course I can say that.
Yes, Jacques. I love you."

Ze end.

Max Stravinsky

Crêpes Suzette

Leon Kampinsky

Ferrrnando Extra Debonnaire

in

MAX IN HOLLYWOOD, BABY

A BELLA BROCCOLI/D.B. DARLING PRODUCTION

Based on an idea by Leon Kampinsky

From a concept by Marcel Proust

Maliciously stolen by Ivan Kazlinsky from Truman Capote

at a martini drenched lunch, Le Côte Basque, December 1952

WRITTEN AND DIRECTED BY MAIRA KALMAN

Production design	M&Co.
Special effects and stunt coordination	EMILY OBERMAN
Hair and makeup	MISS KEIRA ALEXANDRA OSIPOV
Merengue sequence choreographed by	KIRSTEN COYNE
Key Grip	DIDDO RAMM
Edited, edited and edited again by	NANCY PAULSEN
Role of Swifty Lazar played by	CHARLOTTE SHEEDY
Catering	SARA BERMAN
Best Boy	ALEXANDER T. KALMAN
Spiritual Advisor	LULU
Lawsuits pending	MAURICE CHAGALL v. LEON KAMPINSKY
	FEDERICO DE POTATOES v. FERRRNANDO EXTRA DEBONNAIRE
	BELLA BROCCOLI v. D.B. DARLING
	MAX STRAVINSKY v. MAIRA KALMAN
Silent partners and laundered money provided by	VIKING

10 9 8 7 6 5 4 3 2 1

Published by the Penguin Group
Penguin Books USA Inc., 375 Hudson Street, New York, New York 10014, USA
Penguin Books Ltd, 27 Wrights Lane, London W8 5TZ, England
Penguin Books Australia Ltd, Ringwood, Victoria, Australia
Penguin Books Canada Ltd, 10 Alcorn Ave.Toronto, Ontario,Canada M4V 3B2
Penguin Books (N.Z.) Ltd, 182–190 Wairau Road, Auckland 10, New Zealand
Penguin Books, The lost city of Ubur

Penguin Books ltd, Registered Offices: Harmondsworth, Middlesex, England

First published in 1992 by Viking, a division of Penguin Books USA Inc.

Copyright © Maira Kalman, 1992
All rights reserved

Library of Congress Cataloging-in-Publication Data

Kalman, Maira.
  Max in Hollywood / by Maira Kalman.
  Summary: Max the millionaire poet dog and his Parisian dalmatian friend
Crêpes Suzette leave Paris for the lure of glittering Hollywood.
Can movie stardom be far behind?
  ISBN 0-670-84479-9
  [1. Dogs—Fiction. 2. Hollywood (Los Angeles, Calif.)—Fiction.]
I. Title.
PZ7.K1256May 1992
[E]—dc20

91-48200
CIP
AC

Printed in U.S.A.

THE PRODUCERS GRATEFULLY ACKNOWLEDGE THE INVALUABLE ASSISTANCE OF THE FOLLOWING:

The Institute for Advanced Study, Princeton, New Jersey

The Izmir of Zim Zum

Bureau of Cosmetology, Forbidden City, Peking

Filmed on location

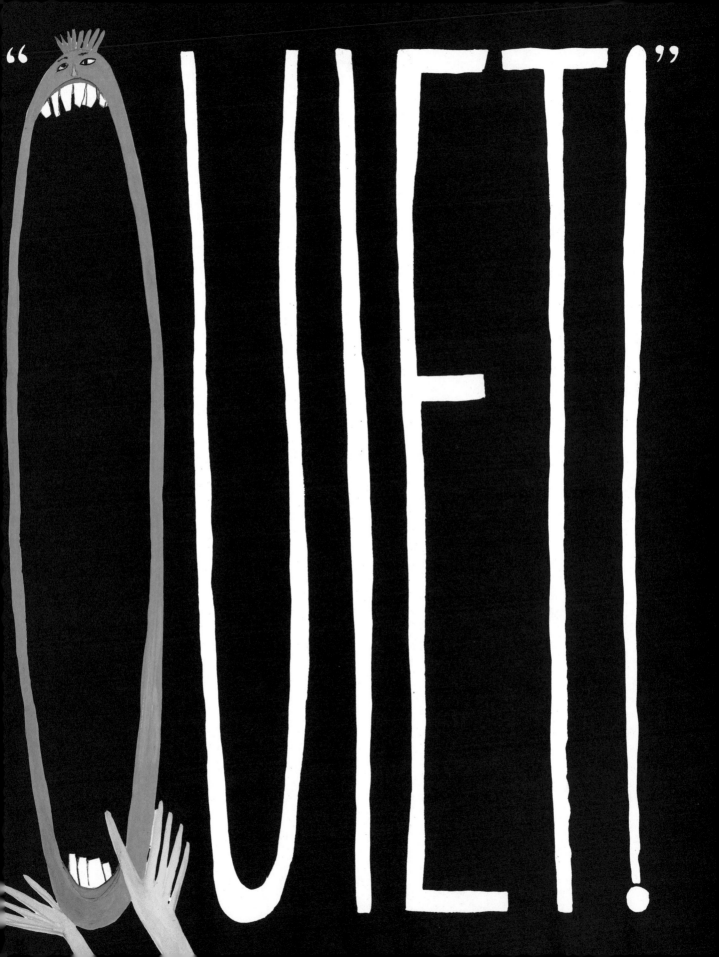

"the izmir of zimzum is dizzy for your fish izzy"

I used to
be just Max.
Poet. Plodder.
Pickleface.
Now I'm in Hollywood
directing a movie.
How did I get here?
On Leon Kampinsky's
beautiful **no**se.
But I might as well
begin at the beginning . . .

[FLASHBACK] to interior of lavish New York apartment. I had just returned from Paris with my bride Crêpes Suzette. The fish clock on the mantel had barely chimed midnight, when a persistent buzzzbuzzz of the buzzer heralded the arrival of a telegram.

ZIPO—GRAM

DEAR MAXIE AND CREPES STOP
WHERE ARE YOU STOP STOP
STOPPING UP THE WORKS STOP
START AT ONCE STOP STOP
SHILLYSHALLYING AROUND STOP
STOP WASTING TIME STOP START
PACKING STOP PULLING OUT ALL
THE STOPS STOP START
STOP START STOP START STOP
LOVE LEON

Were these the
ravings of a madman
or an agent?   **BOTH!**
It was the cigar chomping angel himself,
beckoning us to Hollywood where deals grow on vines.
I was to write and direct a movie. Crêpes was to compose the score.

[CUT] to nervous interlude.
Close-up on Max.
Could this dog handle it?
It's no picnic if you try
something and fail.
What if they make a
monkey out of me?
What if they smell a rat?

Wait.
I'm no chicken.
I can do this. I will do this.
California, here I come.

At the airport we were met by a snappy chappy:

"My name is
Ferrrnando
Extra Debonnaire.

"I have studied at the
Royal Academy of Driving Directors
My face drives them wild,
my directing will drive them mad,
but in the meantime, I just drive.
Life is full of surpreezes, no?
Welcome to L.A. Hop in the stretch.
Are you wearing stretch pants?"

"Watch your step in this town.
There are some back-stabbing,
power-hungry, status-seeking
vegetarians here.
I know of what I speak.
But hey, let's d r i i i v e.
If someplace is close
that means you only drive for
twenty or thirty hours with
your eyes peeled for stars and with
your mouth glued to the phone
yackin and yammerin about
this deal or that script and
faster than you can say
'Marcello Mastroianni
likes to eat salami,'
you have arrived."

We arrived at our hotel. The Garden of Allah. We stood entranced in the midst of a flowering perfumed paradise. Jasmine, honeysuckle, climbing roses. Lemons as big as footballs. Bougainvillea arching up into the turquoise sky.

A fountain sprinkled, birds chirped, swans glided.

**A bellhop showed us into the Hubba-Hubba Suite.
He flashed us a smile and started to sing:**

"Anything you want sir, anything at all
Just press this golden button and give me a call.
You used to be a nobody, an isn't, a not
And now you are a big deal, a someone, a shot.
You used to be a nebbish, a noodle, a fool
And now you're Mr. Big Time with your own private pool.
No order too tall. No excess that can vex us.
We'll treat you like a king, as long as you're a winnah
But if your flick's a flop you'll be whistling for your dinnah."

And with that he tap-danced out of the room.

"Max,"
Crêpes smiled sultrily,
"you know
how to wheestle,
don't you?"

I went to find Leon at poolside. Easier said than done

Pages were pacing around paging people. "Paging

Mr. Popofski." "PAGING MRS.

TUTUTSKI." "Mr. Wiseguy, Mr.

Wisenheimer loves the script." "MR. WISEACRE

MR. WISECRACK THINKS THE SCRIPT SMELLS

LIKE A THREE DAY FISH." At long last I found Leon.

Leon, this life is so lush, so luscious, so luscious-wuscious."

Can the poetry," Leon interrupted. "Save it for the Big

Cheese. They are waiting for us at the studio. Let's go, Maxie."

Back in the car Ferrrnando was rehearsing his directing.
"Baby, could you put more pizzazz in that?" and

"Darling, the camera is not liking you today."

"Yow," he shrieked, "there goes Katharine Hepburn."

It was some trip. We made a right at the giant hat

. . . and a left at the humongous hot dog and there we were . . .

. . . at the gates of Megalomania Studios.
I stared, mesmerized.
Movies . . . A darkened theater.
A raspberry velvet seat. A bag of popcorn.
What more could you ask for?

I'm crazy for movies
I'm weak at the knees
English mysteries,
screwball comedies
Spaghetti westerns
three bowls please
It doesn't matter what, it doesn't matter who
If it's Fred Astaire and Ginger Rogers
It'll absolutely do I worship their allure
If I'm sick, don't find a cure
A Hitchcock scream, a Fellini dream
Film noir, Mel Blanc
And all that's in between
Flood my senses
Make me weep
Kiss the heroine
Kill the creep
The credits, the edits
Houdini! Whodunnits!
Musicals that dance
And dancicals that muse
I'm filled with hope watching Cinemascope
Cause I'm no dope
I love movies.

A booming voice slapped me back to earth:
"WHO WISHES TO PASS THESE PORTALS, SOME MERE MORTALS?
WHAT IS THE SECRET PASSWORD?" the voice demanded.
"Swordfish?" I ventured.
Faster than you could say "star-struck starlet with a seven year itch,"
the gates swung open, and I breezed in like King Vidor.

Feeling as chipper as a kipper I strolled into the white-white room where a secretary was answering ten phones a mile a minute.

"HELLO. No can do. HELLO. He won't see you. HELLO. Lunch at three? HELLO. It's not up to me. HELLO. It's just gossip. HELLO. That's a hot tip. HELLO. Dinner with the Duke. HELLO. Please send up a fluke. HELLO. He wants a cello. HELLO. Just sack that fellow. HELLO. He will. HELLO. He won't. HELLO. He's mad. HELLO. He's livid. HELLO. He says the sky's the limit. HELLO. HELLO. Where have you gone to? HELLO. HELLO. Just get it PRONTO. Hello. GOODBYE. And here's a clue. Don't call us, we'll call you."

She gave me the fish eye.
"You're no Spencah Tracy," she drawled, "but Mr. Darling will see you now."

D.B. Darling

The biggest Darling of them all. Leon and I cringed into the room. But it wasn't a room. It was a **fish**. A roomy fish. A fishy room. A big fat blue fish, a carp to be exact. And like the innocent Pinocchio with his Jiminy Kampinsky, we walked into the mouth of this fish. But this fish was full of water and in the middle, drifting in a canoe, was D.B. and his crew.

Holy mogul!

"Max," he boomed, "obnoxiously happy to see you. Come on over." "You want I should walk on water?" I queried. "Ixnay on the isecrackway," Leon growled. "Just smile and swim." We swam over and soggily sat in the canoe. "Max, we want you to write us a movie. A sugar-smackin, rootin-tootin, high-spy, sci-fi, kissy-kissy, melt-in-your-mouth, madcap musical mystery. A box-office banana— I mean bonanza.

"Can you deliver?" **"Can a snake slither?"** snapped Leon. "Fabuloso. But before you leave I want you to meet your yes-man, Bernie Bennie and your yes-man's yes-man, Diddo." "A yes-man?" I smirked in disbelief. "A yes-man's yes-man?" "Max," D.B. interjected while uncorking a bottle of Chateau-Neuf de Pup, "a yes-man is indispensable in this town and, as everyone knows, two yesses are better than one. Let's toast to that.

EGOS UP."

Ferrrnando was right.
I needed a heavenly slice of hope.
I needed CHEESECAKE.
We zoomed to Cheesecake of the
Stars where the hoi polloi hobnob with
hopefuls and muckety
mucks seduce
swanky stars.

Outside
in the blinding light
I felt dizzy. What was that
lunatic talking about? "Ferrrnando,
do you know any good hideaways?
I'm totally confused." "There's Cafe
Kafka, Mecca for the Miserable. But
you know what Shakespeare said,
'Don't kvetch in the stretch.' Look,
you're no Einstein (or Eisenstein,
for that matter), but ya
havetahavehope."

PSST, HEY BUB, YA WANNA BUY A SCRIPT, CHEAP?

I wolfed down the Carole Lombard
raspberry cheesecake. I polished
off a slice of Gary Cooper. My
stomach was full, but my
head was empty.

Back in the car driving around I saw a billboard:

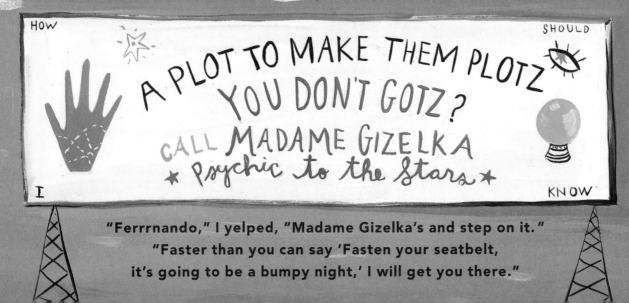

HOW   SHOULD

A PLOT TO MAKE THEM PLOTZ
YOU DON'T GOTZ?
CALL MADAME GIZELKA
* Psychic to the Stars *

I   KNOW

"Ferrrnando," I yelped, "Madame Gizelka's and step on it."
"Faster than you can say 'Fasten your seatbelt,
it's going to be a bumpy night,' I will get you there."

I entered Gizelka's gossamer chamber.

"Hello," I meekly squeaked, "I am. . ."

"No need for introductions, droopy face. I am a psychic. And **you** are a dog in hot water. Listen, tootsie, you're no Orson Welles, but I can help you.

"You're looking for an idea, but are you barking up the wrong tree! In this town all you need are big feet and a hot head...I mean hot feet and a big head...I mean flat feet and a hole in your head...I mean ...oh never mind." She took a pair of yellow gloves and a giant headdress out of a blue box. "Wear these and your power will knock the toupees right off their heads."

The next thing I know she vanishes in a puff of smoke, chanting, "Lassie, Asta, Sparky, this pooch is feeling yucky, I've worked my magic malarkey and now he will be lucky."

Back at the hotel, reactions were mixed.

"Good grief," said Leon. "Why are you wearing a popcorn bucket on your head?" "Dashing wardrobe, darling," smiled Crêpes. "I love it madly," gushed Bernie. "Ditto," gushed Diddo. "This," I explained mystically, "is my magic outfit. Call me Mr. Lucky." "I call you Mr. Idiot," Leon retorted. "Leon, anyone can be normal. But to be an idiot. Now, that's something."

LESS
IS
MORE,
BABY

"Max," Crêpes looked at me pointedly, "be carefool." "Of what?" I asked, admiring myself in the mirror. "Of ze big banana peel, of ze cream pie in your face. Beware."

ME

And so I was ready to write. But there were so many distractions. Massages. Manicures.

Aromatherapy. Acupuncture. Personal trainers. Power lunches. Waterfalls of mineral water.

I met my producer **Bella Broccoli**
who insisted we drink a
brussels sprouts and sauerkraut shake
("the secret of youth, darling")
before each meeting.
We were feted at hotsy-totsy parties
where the swimming pools were
filled with ice cream and
the trees were made out of chocolate.
I was interviewed by
the gossip columnist Billy Sandwich
who linked me romantically
(and ridiculously, I might add)

with Monica Zitti, the tantalizing starlet, who was breathlessly
quoted as saying, "I admire his boots—I mean his boo**k**s."
I bought art. I played tennis and polo and
rode Arabian horses on the beach and
after all this terribly hard work,
I produced a script.

Bernie read it and wept with admiration.

Ditto Diddo.

I showed it to Crêpes,

who was furiously practicing the Bach Carpaccios.

"Max, eet ees flimsy, and superficial.

Zee women are cardboard, zee men are morons.

Zer eez not a soupçon of wit,

no humor, no soul, no intelligence."

"But Crêpes, do you like it?" I asked hopefully.

"Max, eet will lay ze big oeuf."

"You are wrong," I growled. "This script is **perfect**."

"Perfect," sighed Bernie.

"Ditto," dithered Diddo.

VELMA

VIVI

So I started to make my movie. When the script is written, you search the globe for the star. That is called casting. When you have found the absolutely perfect person in every way, you have to change them over *completely*. That is called the makeover. You take a Velma Levine and transform her into *Vivi Divine*. Then the costumes need to be designed. Gowns made from silk illusion. Organza. Plumes. Strapless wonders. Flaring skirts. Tempers flaring. Fittings. Sittings.

Endless, endless, endless meetings.

We're over budget, we're under stress

And all the time they ask of you,

"Mr. Stravinsky, what should we do?

Do you want this, do you want that?

How should we do it? What should we get?"

And all I can think is:

I want more, more, more!

I want pink walls of quilted satin.

I want fresh bagels from Manhattan.

I want more pom-poms on that hat.

I want six legs on that cat.

I want a monogrammed cravat

That says Stravinsky Thought of That.

I want to pout and rant and rave

and get everything I crave

I want to be a celebrity

Have my pawprints in cement for posterity

And just when it seems I have all that I adore

I will graciously implore: I want more I want more I want more.

I won't have conversations, I'll just have monologues.

I won't be simply human, I'll be a demigod.

I will be so eccentric, and they'll still be sycophantic

I will give my opinions to all my harassed minions

Like King Tut with all his plunder,

just like him, how I will thunder

give me more give me more give me more.

I want the whole world to love me

Is that asking very much?

Like the lion in the jungle who devours all his prey

I will tear limb from limb all those who won't obey

and from my gilded throne (which I simply call "just home")

I will regally intone

I want more I want more I want more!

I was broken from my
reverie by a phone call.
Crêpes was waiting for me
at the Waco Taco.

I was ravenous!
"Let me have

two taco tamales

tamales tacquitos

tacquitos burritos

burritos peppito

and make it speedito."

Crêpes was looking at me funny.
"What's wrong, Crêpes?"
"Max, eezer your hat eez shrinking or
your head eez getting bigger."
"That's ridiculous, Crêpes.
It couldn't be. Could it?"

I had to dash back to the set. **Pandemonium.** People racing around with huge **boulders** and thirty-foot shoes. I asked my assistant director (or A.D.) for a cup of **coffee** and a coffeecake. "Tub of toffee and a coughing snake for Mr. Stravinsky," the A.D. yelled to the 2nd A.D. "Mr. Stravinsky's got a bellyache," yelled the 2nd A.D. to the 3rd A.D. **"Mr. Stravinsky** wants maracas to shake," yelled the 3rd A.D. to the 4th A.D. "Cup of coffee and a **coffeecake,** coming right up for Mr. Stravinsky," yelled the 4th A.D. The gaffer, grip and gofer were arguing over a giant **loafer.** Everyone is **yelling.** Tap dancers are rehearsing. Ferrrnando is teaching Leon how to duel. Finally I am ready to direct a scene. **"Quiet,** quiet on the set," my A.D. yells. Lights. Camera. And then as I was about to intone the magic word, the set **froze.** All of Hollywood came to a standstill, poised for the word. T H E   W O R D,

"ACTION."

Then the actors acted. Lights lit. Cameramen filmed. Fake snow fell. Four hundred dancers danced. 60 singers sang. We wove the **magic** spell and then I said the word that brought us back to earth. **"Cut."** The scene was over. The shooting done. "Cut. **Print** and cut the cake." "That's 'check the gate,' Mr. Stravinsky."

BOULDERS

SHOULDERS

COFFEE CAKE

TOFFEE

COUGHING SNAKE

BELLYACHE

MARACAS TO SHAKE

"Right, thanks."

CHECK THE GATE

CUT THE CAKE

FENCY SHMENZERS

FENCERS

DENCERS

GOFER

LOAFER

COFFEECAKE

The next day nobody could do anything right.

Someone told the dancers to **break a leg** and they all broke their legs.

Vivi had **laryngitis** from screaming at her manager; the stunt monkey was threatening to quit unless he got a bigger trailer.

Vino Valentino the heartthrob **fell off** the balcony and started speaking in Chinese.

Ferrrnando was teaching Leon the merengue (which was driving me **insane-gue**) and to top it off, Crêpes was glowering because I said her music was not so hot.

It was time for the big love scene.

"Oh Anastasia, the pink dawn envelops us and as I go to walk my door around the moor . . ."

"CUT" I yelled.

"'Walk my DOOR?'"

"That's what it says in the script, Mr. Stravinsky, 'walk my door.'"

"What nitwit wrote that down? It's 'walk my *dog.*'
DOG! DOG!! DOG!!!
Have you no brains? Have you no eyes? No talent of any kind? I am going mad. Simply mad."
I stormed out leaving the set in stunned silence.

I lay down on my cot. The string quartet I had hired to soothe me played. I dozed off. But the dream was really terrifying. I dreamed that I was in the middle of a vast hall and that everything was falling down around me and I was on a wild horse and that these grotesque gremlins were stomping toward me chanting . . .

"Your head is getting fatter
your ego's on a ladder

going up up up

you great conceited pup
you have nerves of steel
and an iron will
who do you think you are,
Cecil B. de Mille?
Your movie's a disaster
and it's all because of you
The papers will review it
and yell,
'POOCH'S PIC P.U.'"

I jumped up with a yelp. Crêpes was right. My head was the size of a watermelon. The movie was a disaster. What kind of jerk had I become? "A schlemiel," Crêpes (who had obviously been talking to Leon) supplied when she came in. "You have become ze insufferable show-business schmendrick. And you know what? I think we should end zis book right here. Ferrrnando can fix zis fiasco. We must get away from ze madness. And Max, I have something to tell you. . ."

EINSTEIN'S DONUTS

try our box of BLACK HOLES

I was me again.
I looked at Crêpes, cross-eyed with love.
The sky was vast. The night was clear.
I felt on the brink of a grand adventure.
What could it be?

"Yes, yes and yes,"
yessed Bernie. "I don't
agree," said Diddo. "What do you
mean, you don't agree?" "What do
you mean, what do I mean? I'm not sure
that in the big picture that life is full of
surprises. Perhaps everything is foretold."
"Are you saying that fate or some omniscient
being controls our lives? That's ridiculous."
"No, it's not. I would refer you to Schopenhauer and
his treatise *The World as Will and Representation*, in
which he clearly—" "Not the Schopenhauer again, you're
giving me a headache. If I'm wrong, then you have to be
wrong. Wrong, wrong and forever wrong." "You are wrong
to infinity." "You are wrong to the utmost extension of pi."
"You are wronger than the outfit my Aunt Edith
wore to Hilda's engagement party." "I can't top that."

Life is full of surpreezes, no?